SCOUT
THE MIGHTY TUGBOAT

CHARLES BEYL

ALBERT WHITMAN & COMPANY
CHICAGO, ILLINOIS

To Lucas and all the other folks who work
every hour of every day to keep our ports
safe and our shelves stocked
—CB

Library of Congress Cataloging-in-Publication data is on file with the publisher.

Text and illustrations copyright © 2020 by Charles Beyl

First published in the United States of America in 2020 by Albert Whitman & Company

ISBN 978-0-8075-7264-1 (hardcover)

ISBN 978-0-8075-7265-8 (ebook)

Printed in China

10 9 8 7 6 5 4 3 2 1 WKT 24 23 22 21 20

Design by Rick DeMonico

For more information about Albert Whitman & Company,
visit our website at www.albertwhitman.com.

Chug, chug, chug.
Scout the mighty tugboat starts her day
chugging through the waves
on the bright blue water.

Pull, pull, pull.

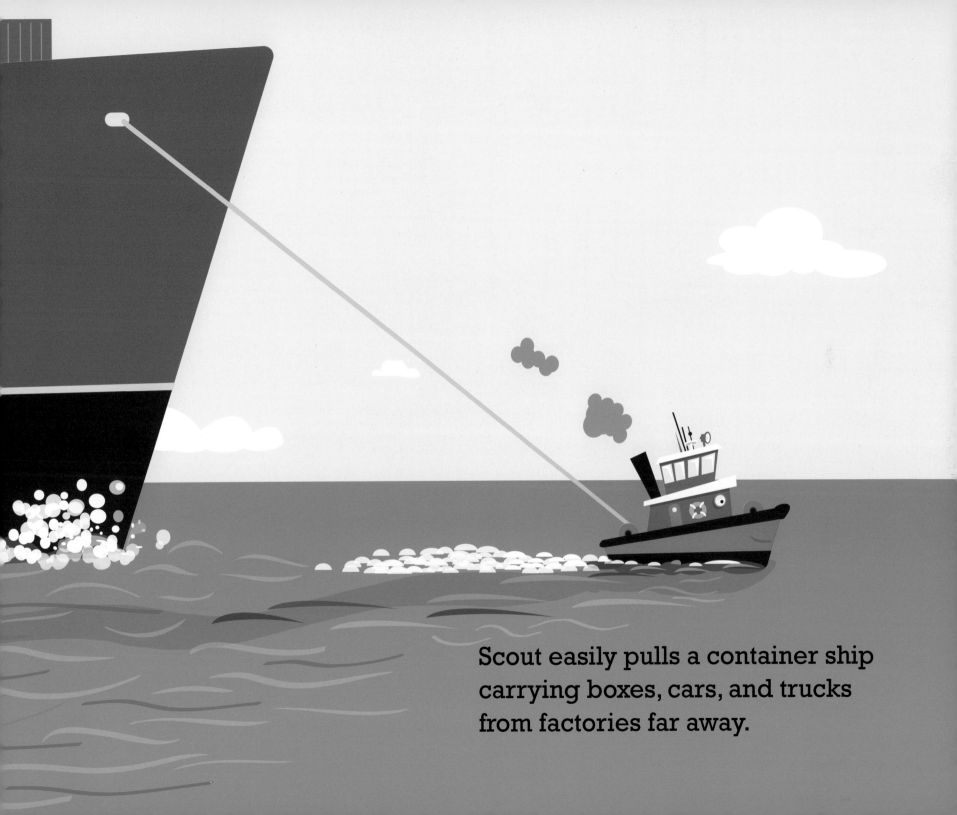

Scout easily pulls a container ship carrying boxes, cars, and trucks from factories far away.

Soar, soar, soar.
White birds soar high over Scout as she brings pink, purple, green, and red containers across the bay.

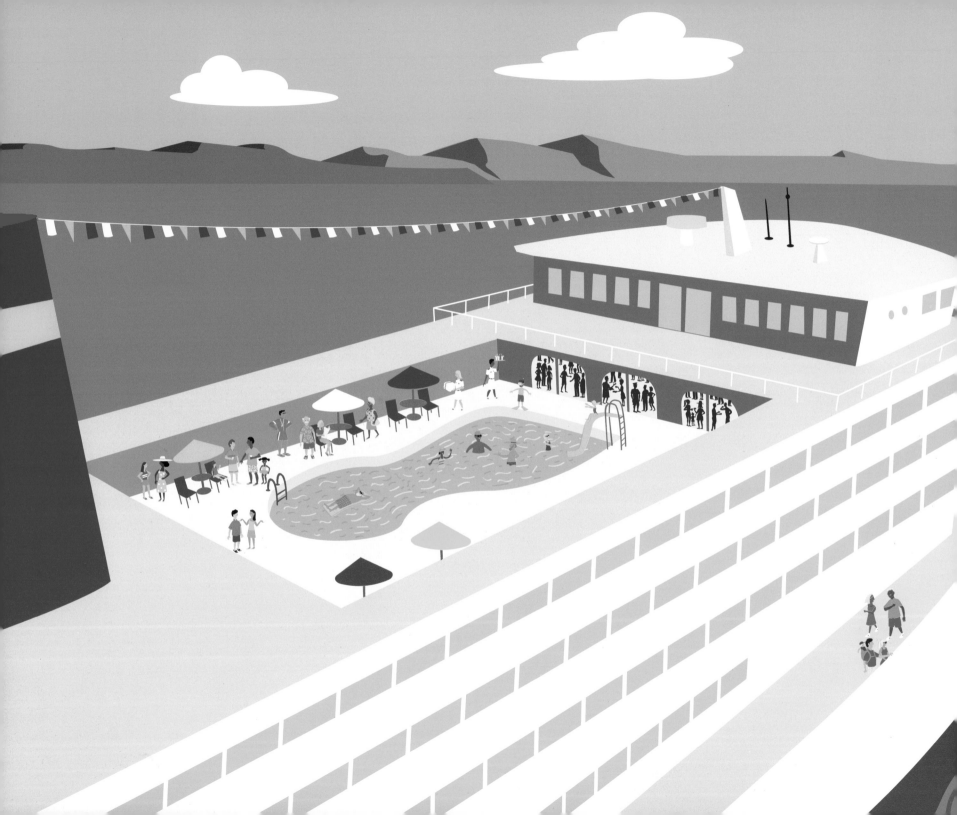

Tow, tow, tow.
Scout uses a strong line
to tow a cruise ship
out to sea.

Push, push, push.
Scout pushes huge tankers
and cargo ships all by herself.

She churns the water,
bubbly and white.

Splash, splash, splash.
Dolphins leap through the waves
Scout makes.

She slides proudly across
the sea after moving the big ships.
Scout can't play today.
There are more ships to move.

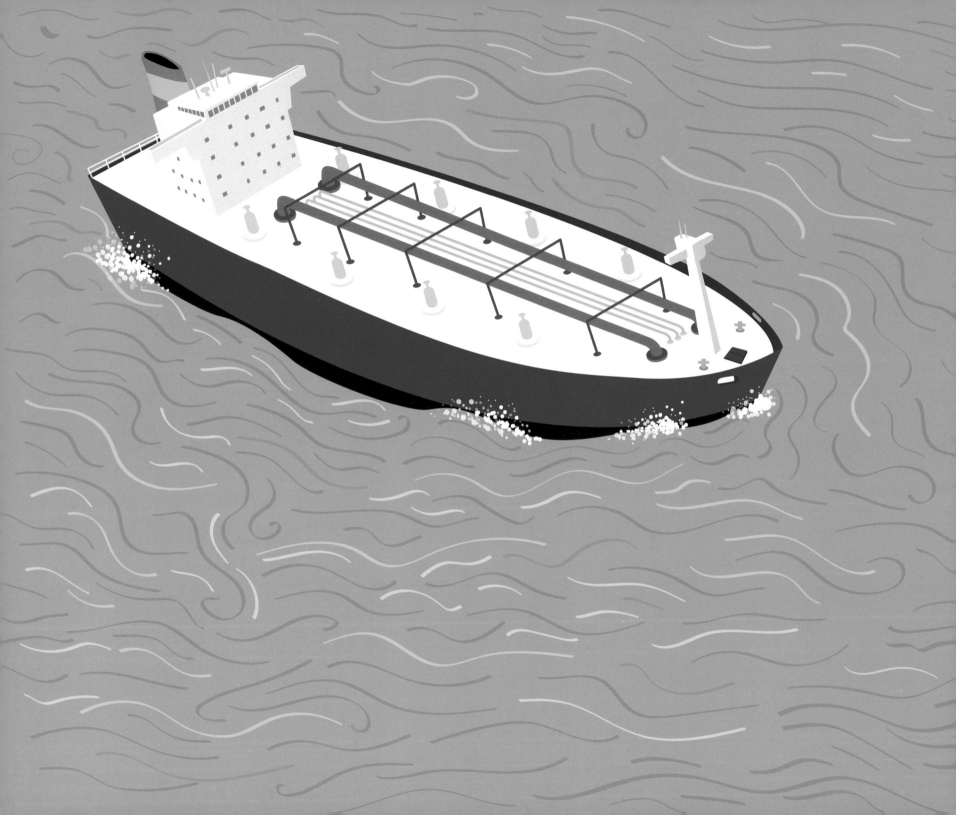

Help, help, help!
On the far side of the bay
an oil tanker's engine won't work.
She is in trouble.

Rumble, rumble, RUUUMMM!
Scout wakes her engines.
Full speed ahead!

"I can do this!" she says
as she races to rescue the big ship.

Push, push, push!
Scout pushes hard.
Harder than she has ever pushed before.

She pushes hard on the starboard side,
hard on the port side, and hard on the stern.

But the tanker is too heavy.
The sharp, black rocks are getting too close.

Scout can't do it alone.
Her tug friends can't be too far away.
Time to radio for help!
"Calling all tugs!
Ship in distress at Lighthouse Point!"

Scout's friends arrive!

Throw lines fast!
Tugs push!
Tugs pull!

Burble, burble, burble...
the bright blue water
churns to white.

Tug, tug, tug.
Scout and her friends
work together, safely guiding the oil tanker
away from the rocks and back to the dock.

Chug, chug, chug.
Scout the mighty tugboat chugs home.
Past pelicans, gulls,
jellyfish, sea turtles, and
the warm, yellow sun...

ending a very busy day on the bay.